Kipper and the Giant

Titles in the series

Kipper and the Giant

Story by Roderick Hunt

Illustrations by Alex Brychta

OXFORD
UNIVERSITY PRESS

Kipper was watching television.

He was watching a programme called

'The angry giant'.

He liked the programme.

The angry giant lived in a castle near
a village.
Nobody in the village liked the giant.
He was always cross.

When the giant was cross he stamped his
feet and the houses shook.

'Oh no!' everyone said.

'He's cross again. He's always cross.'

Kipper went to find Chip but he was out.

He picked up the magic key and it began to glow.

'Ooh!' said Kipper.

He ran to get Biff but she was out with Chip.

The magic began to work.

It took Kipper inside the magic house.

The magic took Kipper to the gate of
the giant's castle.
Kipper was frightened.

He saw a signpost.

It pointed to the village.

He didn't want to meet the giant, so he
went to the village.

Kipper came to the village but it was tiny.

Kipper was a giant.

'Oh no!' said Kipper.

'Go away,' yelled the people.

'We don't want you.

We've got a giant.

We don't want another one.'

The people threw things at Kipper.

'Go away,' they yelled.

'We don't want another giant.

We don't want you.'

'Stop it,' shouted Kipper.

'I'm not a giant. I'm a boy.'

The people said, 'Well, you look like a giant.'

Kipper began to cry.

'I'm not a giant,' he said.

'I'm a little boy and I don't like
this adventure.'

'Giants don't cry,' said the people.

'Perhaps he is a little boy but he looks
like a giant to us.

Perhaps he can help us.'

Kipper helped the villagers to mend
their houses.
He put back the broken roofs.
'Good for Kipper,' everyone said.

'The giant threw this big stone at us,' said
the people.
'We don't want it here.
Can you put it outside the village?'

'Yes,' said Kipper, 'I'll try.'

He picked up the stone and took it

outside the village.

'Good for Kipper!' everyone called.

All the people liked Kipper.

'Thank you,' they said.

'You have helped us a lot.'

The village band played for him.

The giant came back.

He was very angry when he saw Kipper in the village.

'I'm the giant here,' he shouted.

He ran towards the village.

Crash! He fell over the stone.

'Ouch!' he yelled.

The people were frightened but Kipper went
to help the giant.
He picked up the giant's things and put a
bandage round his head.

Kipper was bigger than the giant.

'Be a good giant,' said Kipper.

'Stop being angry and the people will like you.'

So the giant stopped being angry.

'I'll try to be good,' he said.

'Hooray!' shouted the people.

'Let's have a party!'

The key began to glow.

'It's time for me to go now,' said Kipper.

'Goodbye. Thank you for the party.'

The magic took Kipper home.

'Nobody likes an angry giant,' said Kipper.

'What an adventure!'

Questions about the story

- Who went on this Magic Key adventure?
- What had Kipper seen that made the adventure start?
- Why did the people in the village not want Kipper at first?
- What made them change their mind?
- What happened when the giant came back?
- Who was bigger and who was smaller?
- How was the giant different at the end of the story?
- What did Kipper bring back from this adventure?

OXFORD

UNIVERSITY PRESS

Great Clarendon Street, Oxford OX2 6DP

Oxford University Press is a department of the University of Oxford.
It furthers the University's objective of excellence in research, scholarship,
and education by publishing worldwide in

Oxford New York

Athens Auckland Bangkok Bogotá Buenos Aires Calcutta Cape Town
Chennai Dar es Salaam Delhi Florence Hong Kong Istanbul Karachi
Kuala Lumpur Madrid Melbourne Mexico City Mumbai Nairobi
Paris São Paulo Shanghai Singapore Taipei Tokyo Toronto Warsaw

with associated companies in Berlin Ibadan

Oxford is a registered trade mark of Oxford University Press
in the UK and in certain other countries

British Library Cataloguing in Publication Data

Data available

ISBN 0 19 919423 8

Printed in Hong Kong